The Farm Girls'
Revenge

THE FARM GIRLS'
Revenge

Roberta Seiwert Lampe

Tate Publishing & Enterprises

Published by Tate Publishing & Enterprises, LLC
127 E. Trade Center Terrace | Mustang, Oklahoma 73064 USA
1.888.361.9473 | www.tatepublishing.com

Tate Publishing is committed to excellence in the publishing industry. The company reflects the philosophy established by the founders, based on Psalm 68:11,
"The Lord gave the word and great was the company of those who published it."

Book design copyright © 2010 by Tate Publishing, LLC. All rights reserved.
Cover and Interior design by Michael Lee
Illustration by Lauren Judah

Published in the United States of America

ISBN: 978-1-61566-748-2
1. Juvenile Fiction: General
2. Juvenile Fiction: Humorous Stories
10.01.19

WITH SMILES,
AND IN MEMORY
OF MY FUN-LOVING
GRANDMOTHER, GERTRUDE,
AND MY KIND, SWEET, PATIENT
GRANDFATHER, JOSEPH

PRETEND

Pretend you lived back about 1900, when this story took place.

Every day, the girls wore long dresses that often had ruffles on the skirts. The sleeves were long to protect their arms from the sun so their skin would not get brown. The ladies and girls liked their skin to be ivory white. Sunbonnets worn outside protected their faces. Their mothers dressed the same way, except long aprons were worn over their dresses to keep them clean.

The girls hardly ever had their hair cut, as beautiful long hair was a source of pride for them. However, they usually had it braided or rolled up, either at the nape of their neck or around their head.

The boys and men wore loose trousers held up with suspenders or bib overalls. Dark felt hats or summery straw bowlers protected and shielded their eyes from the fierce sun. Their shirts were white or light blue. The sleeves were full and loose so it was easier for them to work. Men's and boys' suits were of heavy black material for Sunday best or for when they needed to go to the village for shopping and visiting.

In the days of this story, there were no cars, no tractors, or huge farm machinery. Horses were used for the farm work and to get wherever the people wanted to go. Bicycles were also ridden by men, women, and children.

Unusual Words in the Story

Beau–sweetheart; boyfriend

Buckboard–farm wagon with carriage seat toward the front and long boards behind for hauling things

Court–pay attention to; wanted to be noticed; to become the other's sweetheart

Dapper–sharply dressed; neat

Granary–farm building where grain was stored

Intentions–tell a girl you are fond of her and perhaps want to be marry her

Love Seat or Settee–a small sofa for two people

Molasses–a thick syrup-like spread for bread or for baking

Parlor–a special, fancier living room

Smitten–really like someone; love struck

Suitor–a boy or man who wanted to date a girl; to be a boyfriend

The Smitten Neighbor Boys

Gertrude heard the dog bark. Horses snorted and stomped their hooves.

She looked at her sister, Mary, and scowled. "Do you think that is the brothers again?"

Mary gingerly pushed the lace parlor curtain to the side and peeked out. "You are right, Gertrude; them and their noisy buckboard." She flopped down on the nearby settee and divulged into laughter. "They caught poor Papa in the yard. You know what they want, and it is not to buy seed wheat." Mary laughed more. "They are here to look over Papa's girls."

Gertrude sank down on the burgundy

velvet love seat, patted the plush curved back, and giggled. "Wouldn't those two like to sit here and court us?"

"I do not think that is going to happen," quipped Mary. "We have to think of some way to discourage them."

"You know why they are interested in us." Gertrude sighed. "They think Papa has lots of money. That is why they are always over here talking to him."

Mary grinned. "That is only one reason. They see Papa with nine daughters and only one son. They know all of us girls have to help with the farm work, in the fields, and around the cattle and horses. It's no secret we can all handle the horses, Gertrude." Mary giggled real ornery. "And every one of us can milk a cow and feed the baby calves." She wrapped her arms tightly around herself and gazed dreamily across the room. "We don't like to slop the hogs, but we do it."

Gertrude turned serious. "We are good with horses, aren't we?" She stood up. "That is the way it is done in the old country: the women do the work, and the men sit on the edge of the field and watch. Those neighbor boys still like to think it should work here like it does in Germany." She shook her head and added sarcastically, "They have all those boys in that family but no sisters to do the work." She screwed up her face in disgust. "So they are out trying to court girls who are used to doing heavy farm work. They are not really looking for wives, but work horses."

Mary laughed. "Sister, dear, you are so hilarious, but right. We have to think of a way to get them out of our hair." A stern look came over her face; then a bright idea dawned.

"Maybe there is a way." Mary cautiously pushed the curtain aside again. "They are with Papa, walking to the barn. Papa probably told them about the twin calves Old Nelly had." She grabbed Gertrude's hand. "Come on; I think this will work. They are not going to trick us that easy."

The sisters watched their chance then ran out the door. Used to hiking up their long skirts, they wasted no time getting up on the men's wagon.

"Let me drive," ordered Gertrude. "You get on the tailgate and get ready to jump when I yell 'Now.'"

Gertrude grabbed the reins, slapped the horses across the rumps and screamed, "Giddyup." The startled horses took off like a shot.

"Where are we going?" demanded Mary. A delighted smirk lit up her face.

"You will see." Gertrude laughed. She pulled the reins to the left. The horses shot past the granary and through the pasture gate. The buckboard bounced over the rough clumps of pasture grass as Gertrude hung on tightly to the seat. With the quick, deft movements of a rowdy farm girl, she bundled her skirt under one arm. Twisting around, she swung her legs over the bench.

Still hanging on the reins, she guided the horses to the pond. With them headed in the right direction, she dropped the lines and scrambled back by Mary. Scared by the rattling and rumbling of the noisy wooden wagon, and the girls' shouting and wild, hilarious laughter, the horses headed right down into the pond as far as they could go.

"Now!" Gertrude shouted. Together, the sisters tumbled off the end of the wagon and rolled in the heavy grass. "We did it." She giggled.

"Shhh," Mary whispered. "I hear the men yelling. Stay down low so they do not see us."

The girls halfway stood up and looked for the tallest grass. "Over there." Mary motioned. Stooping low, they slipped through clumps of tall bluestem. A good distance from the pond, they sank down, buried their faces between their knees, and covered their dark hair with their hands.

The brothers heard the racket as the wagon rumbled past the barn. The dog barked up a storm then growled and barked more. He took off at a dead run toward the pasture. The men ran to the barn door and could hardly believe what they did not see.

"Our wagon is gone!" John shouted. "The dog is heading out to the pond."

The three men took off running. "There is the wagon, sticking out of the pond," stammered Jake.

Papa had to slow down to a walk. He watched the goings-on with amusement. He knew several of his more willful daughters must have had a hand in this.

"What made them run?" the youngest brother demanded. "Those horses never spook."

The older brother, Jake, bounded up on the exposed tailgate and started talking softly and slowly to the horses. The animals shuffled around uneasily in the soft pond bottom. Carefully, Jake crawled forward until he could grab the lines and settle down the frightened animals. He was finally able to lead the horses through the pond and out the other side.

Papa caught up with them, all tuckered out and short of breath. "The horses and wagon do not look any worse for the runaway."

"No," snarled John, "it was probably that dog of yours. He has never liked our team."

Jake looked at Papa then managed to sputter, "I think we had better go home.

The horses need to be settled and brushed down." He grinned. "We will come back another day to look at the calves." Then he winked at Papa and chuckled. "And if any of your daughters are around, we would like to look at them, too."

"Yeah," Papa answered. He grimaced as the neighbor boys drove the team out of the pasture, through the yard, and down the road.

"Yeah, yeah," he muttered. Just then he saw some of the grass move, and his two most strong-headed daughters stood up. He shook his head and scolded, "Ach, meine kinder, was ist dis?" ("Oh, my children, what is this?") A wide smile spread across his face; then he doubled over in laughter. "Oh, my girls. What girls you are."

The girls linked their arms through his, and the three headed back to the house.

"Guess we slowed those two down, at least for today." Mary giggled.

"This will not cure them," snorted Gertrude snidely. "Those brothers just never give up. They will be back."

"Then we will be ready and waiting. I already have a perfect plan that is sure to discourage them." Mary rubbed her hands together in glee.

"I hope so," whispered Gertrude thoughtfully. "I have my eye on sweet Joseph."

Papa smiled at her. "He would make a good husband for you, Gertrude. His calm, easygoing manner would slow down your wild, rowdy nature." Papa squeezed her arm gently. "I see the way he looks at you in church. You must be nicer to him, though, than you have been to the neighbor boys."

Mary prodded Gertrude. "Why not tell Papa what Joseph's sister told you."

Gertrude blushed.

"What, Gertrude? Why do you blush? Has Joseph made his intentions known to you?"

"Oh, Papa, it was just a story his sister told me. I am not sure it is even true."

Gertrude looked down at her hands then looked at Mary from under lowered eyelids.

"Oh, Gertrude, the story is so sweet. It

would just thrill me if my secret beau's sister told me the same story. Tell Papa. He will like to hear it."

Papa and the girls needed a rest after all the excitement, so they sat on the wooden glider by the front porch.

Gertrude looked at Papa, blushed a bit more, then cleared her throat. "Joseph's sister told me he was coming to see me last week. He did not want to tell any of his family where he was going. You know how shy he is." She smiled to herself. "He was riding his bicycle to come. That is four miles, is it not, Papa?"

Papa nodded.

"I think their farm is at the top of a hill," she said. "And the hill slants down rather steeply."

Papa nodded again.

"She said there were some terrible deep ruts in the road. Joseph really got his bicycle going downhill. Then the chain broke. He could not stop because he had no brakes." Gertrude leaned against Papa for a long time. "The road was so rough, Papa. He hit one of those ruts in the trail. Joseph's bicycle started wobbling all over. It hit one of those deep furrows and just headed off across the road and ran right into a tree." Tears welled in Gertrude's eyes. "Poor Joseph; he was so embarrassed. He was not hurt, but his Sunday suit got all dirty. He knew he had to walk back to the farm to get his older brother to help him." She stopped for a few seconds then added, "Oh, my poor dear Joseph."

"He will make it over here to court you, Gertrude," Mary went on, teasingly. "In the meantime, we need to figure out how to get rid of the pesky neighbor boys. That way Joseph can come and not have to compete for your affection." She put her arm around her sister's shoulder.

The sisters' prediction did come true. Within the week, the smitten suitors returned. All decked out in their Sunday suits and smart black hats, they strutted around like peacocks with their tail feathers spread out in glorious display.

"Just came to show you our new buggy," gushed Jake. "The seats are soft leather, the finest kind. Do you think your daughters would like to join us on a Sunday-afternoon ride?"

"I am not sure," Papa answered. "They are in the house resting. Why not come to the barn and see the new calves." Papa grinned as he shook his head. "It is hard to believe they have grown so much since the last time you were here. Old Nelly is such a good milk cow. She has always raised good calves."

John chuckled. "Sure, why not. If the girls see our shiny buggy, how will they be able to resist?" He motioned to Jake. "Let's go see the calves first." The two followed Papa to the barn.

But Papa's two willful daughters were not resting. They had watched the whole scene from the parlor window. Grinning like Cheshire cats, they headed for the kitchen cabinet and Mama's jars of thick dark molasses and mustard.

"Get the cornmeal, Mary." She pulled the sack out from the lower shelf.

"Hurry up, Gertrude; they followed Papa to the barn." Mary hissed, "It is now or never." The sisters dashed out the back door.

Sneaking around the front of the buggy, Mary slithered up around the fancy seats. "Hand me the jars."

With quick, deft swipes of her hand, the seats were slathered and coated with molasses and mustard. Several handfuls of cornmeal finished off the concoction.

"Come on; hurry up," snarled Gertrude nervously.

The two tricksters raced for the house. Taking two steps at a time, they scurried up the back stairs to their bedroom. Slamming down on the bed laughing, they buried their heads down deep in the featherbed so Mama would not hear them. They did not want their sisters or brother to know what had been done. No witnesses or stories could be spread about what had taken place. Their innocence had to be protected.

The dapper gentlemen walked back to their buggy to show it off and impress Papa. One look at the wonderful leather seats, and they exploded.

John shook his fist in Papa's face and sneered. "Is this the way your daughters hope to gain suitors? They should have to live out their lives as old maids after doing something like this." He stomped his foot hard on the ground. "You can tell your precious daughters they will never see us again."

Jake rubbed his hands over the soft leather. "Molasses…mustard." He grabbed an immaculate white starched handkerchief from his breast pocket and began rubbing. "How are we ever going to get this clean?"

Papa bit his lip to hide his amusement. His daughters had been at it again. After this story got out, their suitors would indeed be scarce. Maybe the neighbor boys would be too embarrassed to tell other fellows what had happened to their fancy buggy.

The next Sunday, Joseph strolled down the aisle of the little country church and sat down in the pew in front of Gertrude and Mary. He turned around and smiled shyly at the girls. His eyes twinkled with merriment.

But he was still to shy to talk to Gertrude after the service. A group of farm boys gathered outside under a big oak tree. Joseph inched his way into the center of the group, hiding.

Back home, the sisters rushed upstairs and flopped down on their beds. The springs squeaked loudly.

"Shh, Mary; settle down."

"Oh, Gertrude," gushed Mary, "did you see Joseph? The middle part in his curly dark hair was just perfect!" She giggled. "And he is so cute because he is too scared to talk to you."

Gertrude blushed. "Shh, Mama will hear." Then she grinned at her sister and whispered, "I love his handlebar mustache."

She giggled then hid her head in the fluffy goose-down feather pillow.

But Joseph was not quite as quiet and easily embarrassed as the girls thought. Late in the afternoon, Joseph walked up the front walk to the girls' house. He noticed the porch swing at one end of the long, wide veranda. A light knock on the door awoke the big, sleek-haired dog under the front porch. He came out growling and barking.

Joseph ignored the noisy mutt and kept on knocking. The harder he knocked, the louder the dog barked.

Mary rolled off the bed and looked out the upstairs window. "Gertrude, Gertrude, get up. Brush your hair and straighten your blouse and skirt. Hurry up, hurry up."

"Quiet," growled Gertrude. She rolled the pillow over her head.

"Get up, Sister. Your special beau is here." Mary pulled the pillow away from Gertrude's head. "He fixed his bicycle." She laughed hilariously. "And he missed all the ruts in the road. And he missed hitting the trees." She shrieked, "He's here, he's here."

"Who? Who is here?"

"Joseph, silly sister. Joseph is here."

Gertrude jumped off the bed, rubbed her hands over her clothes, and brushed her dark hair back from her face. "He is here? You are fibbing." She stumbled toward the window.

"Oh my!" She flew down the stairs and beat her mama to the door. Pulling the door open, she gushed, "Joseph, hello." A touch of pink spread over her cheeks. Trying to be more ladylike, she whispered much softer, "Why, hello, Joseph."

"Hello, Gertrude." He rubbed the ends of his handlebar mustache nervously. "I hope you do not mind."

"Oh no, not at all." She smiled sweetly. "Come; let us sit on the swing. It is nice and cool there in the shade." Pulling her thick skirt closer to herself, she wondered what to say next. Then, finally, a few words tumbled out. "You have your bicycle fixed, I see." She hoped she did not sound too forward.

"Yes." Joseph's eyes twinkled. "Surely you will not drive it into the pond." A deep chuckle rumbled from his chest. A serious look crossed his face. "And, Gertrude, my bicycle seat is not fine leather." His merry laughter caused her to look at him more fully. "And it is not big enough to bother getting out the molasses and mustard jars." Joseph laughed more heartily then.

"You heard?" gasped Gertrude.

"Everyone knows. You and Mary are known as the 'Sticky Mess Girls.'" Joseph laughed again. "You know those neighbor boys of yours could not pass up the chance to let everyone know what you terrible girls did to their fancy buggy." He smiled ever so kindly. "It was their way of letting all the rest of us know they could afford such a fine buggy." He touched Gertrude's hand softly. "And that is why I am here. I like a girl with lots of spunk."

"Oh my," she muttered.

Joseph was not discouraged. Every Sunday, even through rain and snow, he came. His bicycle chain broke several times over the next months. But he was always able to coast down the long hill by missing all the ruts in the road. And he never hit another tree in a fence row.

He laughed with Gertrude's mama and sisters, and charmed her papa. The girls did not mess up his bicycle. They never covered his bicycle seat with a sticky cornmeal goo.

After a year, he felt safe. He came one Sunday afternoon and stopped at the front gate. Joseph was driving a fine buggy with soft leather seats. A team of well-brushed black horses stood patiently while Joseph walked up to the front door.

"May I have your daughter's hand in marriage?" he asked Gertrude's papa.

"If Gertrude wills it," Papa answered.

Joseph and Gertrude walked down the aisle of that little church to be married on May 9, 1905.

BIOGRAPHY

In the mid-1990s, Roberta Seiwert Lampe's family battled an onslaught of health and tragic problems. Her husband fought cancer and chemo; her mother's health problems ended with her eventual death; and her daughters faced terrific accidents and trials. The author struggled to be the mainstay of support for each of them.

Eventually, the hardships pressured her. It also provided her with the impetus to put her stories on paper. Prior to that, the time just never seemed right.

In the midst of all the crises, she awoke one morning to hear her subconscious say, "The time is now." She lifted a worn business advertising pen from the desk drawer, grabbed a wad of scratch paper, and set about follow the directive. Wherever she went, the old pen and paper were along and handy.

The pen, its advertising logo already dim, appeared to be almost out of ink when she began. However, it was a magical pen. Whenever it touched the paper, her subconscious asserted itself. The words came in torrents, and what appeared surprised even her. After two and a half years, she had penned two lengthy novels and nine short children's stories, all in long hand.

The magic of the pen lasted on. It was only after the last words of the many stories were written that the old orange and black pen finally ran out of ink and gave up the ghost. One reader suggested that perhaps the angels kept filling the ink supply, as the author certainly never did.

The pen, paper, and words helped the author, and gave her the emotional stamina to carry on.

listen|imagine|vie.w|experience

AUDIO BOOK DOWNLOAD INCLUDED WITH THIS BOOK!

In your hands you hold a complete digital entertainment package. In addition to the paper version, you receive a free download of the audio version of this book. Simply use the code listed below when visiting our website. Once downloaded to your computer, you can listen to the book through your computer's speakers, burn it to an audio CD or save the file to your portable music device (such as Apple's popular iPod) and listen on the go!

How to get your free audio book digital download:

1. Visit www.tatepublishing.com and click on the e|LIVE logo on the home page.
2. Enter the following coupon code:
   6ad8-3d21-5680-347a-3b24-4806-1afe-7955
3. Download the audio book from your e|LIVE digital locker and begin enjoying your new digital entertainment package today!